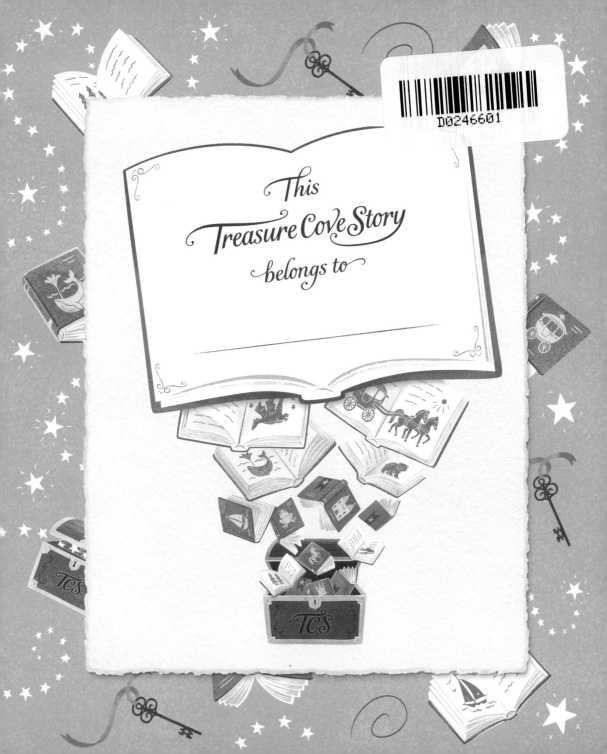

This
Treasure Cove Story
belongs to

LOOK OUT FOR MATER!

A CENTUM BOOK 978-1-912396-80-1
Published in Great Britain by Centum Books Ltd.
This edition published 2018.

1 3 5 7 9 10 8 6 4 2

Centum Books Ltd, 20 Devon Square, Newton Abbot,
Devon, TQ12 2HR, UK.

www.centumbooksltd.co.uk | books@centumbooksltd.co.uk
CENTUM BOOKS Limited Reg. No. 07641486.

A CIP catalogue record for this book is available
from the British Library.

Printed in China.

centum

A Treasure Cove Story

Disney · PIXAR
THE WORLD OF
Cars

Look Out for Mater!

Adapted by Andrea Posner-Sanchez
Illustrated by Ivan Boix Estudi

*T*imes had changed in Radiator Springs. Once it was a sleepy little town. Now cars came from all over the world to visit the new racing headquarters of Lightning McQueen. The famous race car liked all the attention he got from his fans. But what he really enjoyed was spending time with his new friends.

Lightning's two closest friends were Mater and Sally.

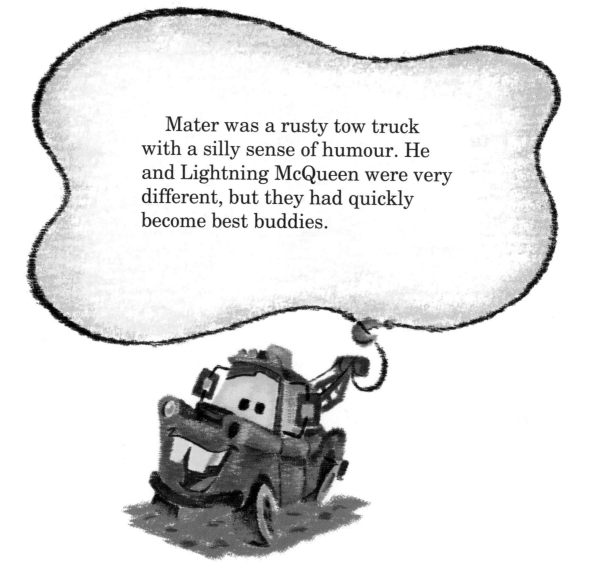

Mater was a rusty tow truck with a silly sense of humour. He and Lightning McQueen were very different, but they had quickly become best buddies.

Sally was Lightning's 'girlyfriend', as
Mater often said. She was caring and smart.
Lightning loved driving around with Sally
by his side.

One day, Sally and Lightning drove to a cliff overlooking a gravel pit. 'That seems like a fun place to race,' said Lightning. 'I'll have to bring Mater there.'

'Please don't,' Sally begged. 'I'm always warning Mater that this place is dangerous. I don't want to worry while I'm out of town for the next few days. Promise me you'll look out for Mater while I'm away.'

GRAVEL PIT

Back in town, Lightning was sadly rolling along Main Street when Mater came up beside him.

'Aw, shoot! Are you moping 'cause Miss Sally went away?' Mater asked his friend. 'You need some Mater-style fu-un!'

Even though Lightning wasn't in the
mood, he knew he'd better go along.
After all, he had promised Sally
he would look out for Mater.

Before long,
Mater was speeding
towards a grassy hill.
'Slow down!' yelled
Lightning. But Mater
kept on going. The
tow truck honked
his horn and flew
over the hill with
a big grin.

Next, Mater drove down a winding dirt road – backwards!

'You're crazy!' Lightning called to him. 'Turn around!'

'Nah, it's more fun when you're looking the other way,' Mater said, chuckling.

As the sun began to set, Mater insisted
on going to one last place - the gravel pit!
'We can't go down there,' Lightning said.
'I promised Sally...'

Before the race car could even finish his sentence, Mater was revving his engine and speeding around the pit.

'Come on down!' cried Mater. 'This is fu-un!'

KEEP OUT

Lightning realized
that if he wanted to
look out for Mater, he
had better stay close
to him. So the race
car slowly inched
his way down the
slippery slope.

Mater rushed
by, leaving Lightning
behind in a cloud
of dust.

Just then, the two friends heard a loud 'Ahem!'
An angry bulldozer was coming up behind them.
'Stop messing up my gravel!' he yelled. 'This pit
is not for playing in!'

Gulp! 'Guess it's time to go!' cried Lightning.
'Right behind ya, buddy,' replied Mater.

The next day, Mater had a surprise for his friend. Lightning followed Mater to... the gravel pit.

'No way!' shouted Lightning. 'Let's find a safe place to have fun.'

GRAVEL PIT

'Shhh,' whispered Mater as he rolled past the snoring bulldozer. 'Big Bull's sleeping. And anyways, this time we won't even *touch* the gravel.'

Before Lightning could stop him, Mater rode
onto some rails that had been set up to help move
gravel from one end of the pit to the other. The
race car watched as Mater zoomed up and down
the rails with a big smile on his face.
The tow truck honked and hooted
as he whooshed around the turns.

Lightning knew he should stop Mater
– he had promised Sally.
But it looked like such fun!
Lightning had to try, too.

Lightning made his
way to the top of the track.
He revved his engine and
took off. *'Ka-chow!'* It was
fantastic!

'I told ya it was fu-un!'
Mater yelled.

'But Sally's right about
this place being dangerous,'
said Lightning. 'Let's get
going before something
goes wrong.'

But as the sun began to set, Mater insisted on one more ride. After a while, there was a loud *thwack!*

'You okay, buddy?' Lightning called into the darkness.

Suddenly, a floodlight lit the gravel pit. A booming voice shouted, 'What is going on here?' Big Bull had woken up to find Mater hanging by his tow cable!

Luckily, Mater wasn't hurt. But he was stuck. 'I can get you down,' Big Bull fumed. 'But I'll have to break your tow cable to do it.'

Once Mater was free, he was as quiet as could be. What kind of tow truck was he without his cable?

Lightning felt bad, too. He should have done a better job of looking out for Mater.

The next night, Sally came back to town.
'Mater, what happened to you?' she gasped.
When she found out that he and Lightning
McQueen had been in the gravel pit, she was
very angry.

'Lightning tried to warn me,' said Mater.
'I shoulda been a better friend and listened
to him.' He started to cry.

'You could have really been hurt,' Sally said.
'Thankfully, we can get that tow cable fixed.'
Mater smiled and turned to his red friend.
'Then we can go out for more Mater-style
fu-un!'
Sally frowned. Lightning couldn't help
laughing. 'This time, I pick the place. I'll show
you how to have Lightning McQueen-style fun
– *without* getting hurt!'

Treasure Cove Stories

Book list may be subject to change.